Hey Merry Maker!
Wishing you a holiday season as warm and cozy as your favorite Christmas sweater!

Feel the warmth of the season with every color, as you create your own little winter wonderland filled with love, joy, and sparkle. Whether it's a snowy afternoon or a quiet evening by the fireplace, this book is here to bring you comfort and inspiration.

> Very important! Please use a blank sheet of paper between the pages to prevent marker bleed-through.

Thank you for your purchase

If you'd like to share your beautiful creations, I'd be so excited to see them! Just mention @katherinehendrickart in your posts, and I'd love to showcase your amazing artwork in my Stories. Let's spread some holiday magic together!

instagram.com/katherinehendrickart
or
tiktok.com/@katherinehendrickart

Yours sincerely, Katherine

https://katherinehendrick.com/

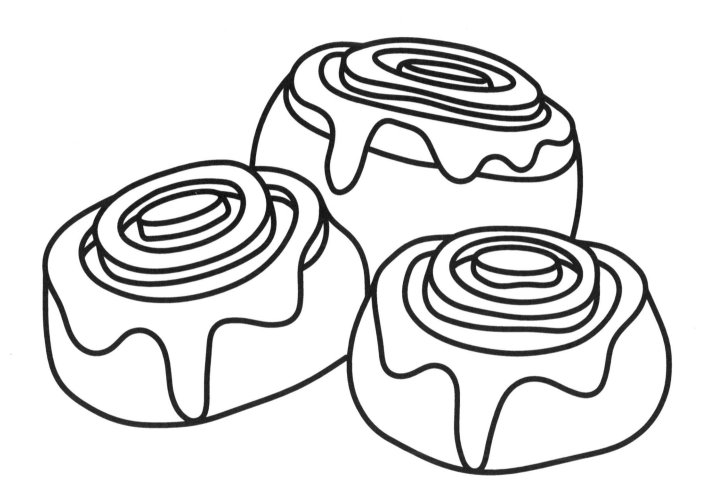

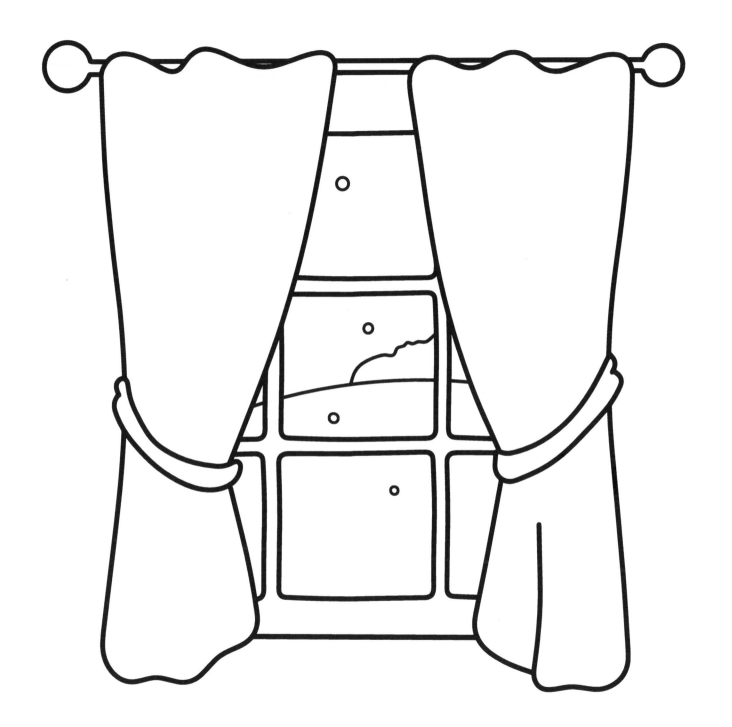